See the Colors
Sign Language for Colors

by Dawn Babb Prochovnic
illustrated by Stephanie Bauer

Content Consultant:
William Vicars, EdD, Director of Lifeprint Institute
and Associate Professor, ASL & Deaf Studies
California State University, Sacramento

magic wagon

visit us at www.abdopublishing.com

For Katia, who colors my world with smiles and laughter—DP
In memory of my grandmother Lucy, who lived a long and lovely 97 years with 5 children,
16 grandchildren, 38 great-grandchildren, and 10 great-great grandchildren—SB

Published by Magic Wagon, a division of the ABDO Group, 8000 West 78th Street, Edina, Minnesota 55439.

Printed in the United States.

 PRINTED ON RECYCLED PAPER

Written by Dawn Babb Prochovnic
Illustrations by Stephanie Bauer
Edited by Stephanie Hedlund and Rochelle Baltzer
Cover and Interior layout and design by Neil Klinepier

Story Time with Signs & Rhymes provides an introduction to ASL vocabulary through stories that are written and structured in English. ASL is a separate language with its own structure. Just as there are personal and regional variations in spoken and written languages, there are similar variations in sign language.

Library of Congress Cataloging-in-Publication Data

Prochovnic, Dawn Babb.
  See the colors : sign language for colors / by Dawn Babb Prochovnic ; illustrated by Stephanie Bauer ; content consultant, William Vicars.
    p. cm. -- (Story time with signs & rhymes)
  Includes "alphabet handshapes;" American Sign Language glossary, fun facts, and activities; further reading and web sites.
  ISBN 978-1-60270-671-2
  [1. Stories in rhyme. 2. Color--Fiction. 3. Gardening--Fiction. 4. American Sign Language. 5. Vocabulary.] I. Bauer, Stephanie, ill. II. Title.
  PZ8.3.P93654See 2009
  [E]--dc22
                                                        2009002405

Alphabet Handshapes

American Sign Language (ASL) is a visual language that uses handshapes, movements, and facial expressions. Sometimes people spell English words by making the handshape for each letter in the word they want to sign. This is called fingerspelling. The pictures below show the handshapes for each letter in the manual alphabet.

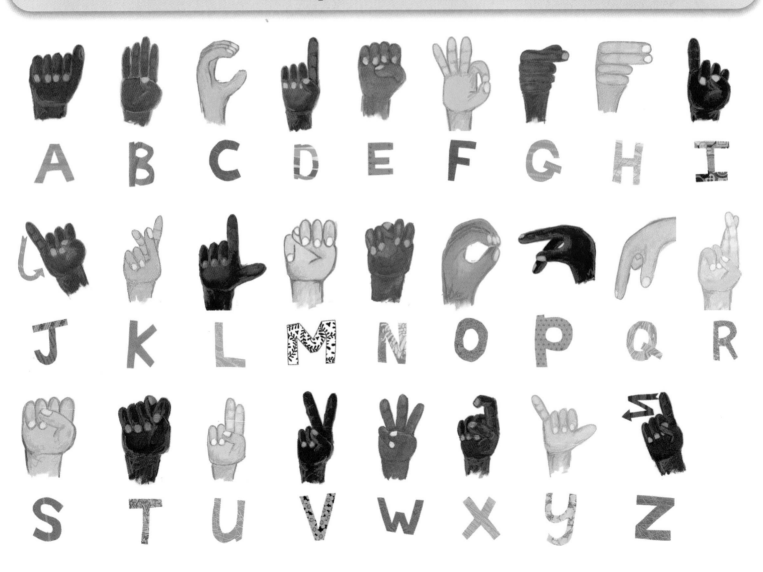

See the **colors**, see the **colors**, see the **colors**, little one.
See the **colors** of our garden. See the **colors**, little one.

colors

5

See the **yellow**, see the **yellow**, see the **yellow**, little one.
Greet the **yellow** morning sunshine. See the **yellow**, little one.

yellow

See the **brown**, see the **brown**, see the **brown**, little one.
Dig the **brown** dirt with your shovel. See the **brown**, little one.

brown

See the **green**, see the **green**, see the **green**, little one.
Soak the **green** leaves needing water. See the **green**, little one.

10

green

See the **pink**, see the **pink**, see the **pink**, little one.
Smell the **pink** blooms bursting open. See the **pink**, little one.

pink

13

See the **red**, see the **red**, see the **red**, little one.
Pick the **red** fruit we are growing. See the **red**, little one.

red

15

See the **blue**, see the **blue**, see the **blue**, little one.
Chase the **blue** jays from our garden. See the **blue**, little one.

blue

See the **white**, see the **white**, see the **white**, little one.
Dance with **white** silk dandelions. See the **white**, little one.

18

white

See the **purple**, see the **purple**, see the **purple**, little one.
Taste the juicy **purple** berries. See the **purple**, little one.

purple

See the **orange**, see the **orange**, see the **orange**, little one.
Watch the **orange** evening sunset. See the **orange**, little one.

orange

23

See the **colors**, see the **colors**, see the **colors**, little one.
Share the **colors** from our garden. See the **colors**, little one.

24

colors

See the **black**, see the **black**, see the **black**, little one.
Hush, the **black** night hides the colors. See the **black**, little one.

black

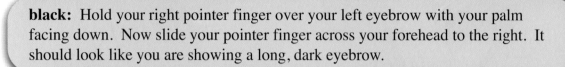

American Sign Language Glossary

black: Hold your right pointer finger over your left eyebrow with your palm facing down. Now slide your pointer finger across your forehead to the right. It should look like you are showing a long, dark eyebrow.

blue: Hold your "B Hand" in front of you and quickly twist your hand from side to side a couple of times.

brown: Touch your "B Hand" to your cheek, then slide your hand down to your jaw. It should look like you are showing where a beard grows.

colors: Hold your hand near your chin with your palm facing in, then wiggle or flutter the tips of your fingers against your chin. It should look like your fingers represent a shimmering rainbow of colors.

green: Hold your "G Hand" in front of you and quickly twist your hand from side to side a couple of times.

orange: Hold your "C Hand" near your mouth then close and open your fist several times alternating from a "C Hand" to an "S Hand." It should look like you are squeezing an orange.

pink: Hold your "P Hand" in front of your mouth and brush your middle finger down your lips to your chin. This sign is related to the sign for "red."

purple: Hold your "P Hand" in front of you and quickly twist your hand from side to side a couple of times.

red: Point to your lips with your pointer finger then brush your finger down your lips to your chin. It should look like you are pointing to your red lips.

white: Touch the palm of your hand to your chest then pull your hand away from your chest and press your fingers to your thumb. It should look like you are grabbing the front of your white T-shirt.

yellow: Hold your "Y Hand" in front of you and quickly twist your hand from side to side a couple of times.

Fun Facts about ASL

If you know you are going to repeat a fingerspelled word during a conversation or story, you can fingerspell it the first time, then quickly show a related ASL sign to use when the word comes up again. For example, you can fingerspell L-A-V-E-N-D-E-R, then sign "purple" since lavender is a hue of purple. This shows your signing partner that you mean "lavender" the next time you sign "purple."

Most sign language dictionaries describe how a sign looks for a right-handed signer. If you are left-handed, you would modify the instructions so the signs feel more comfortable to you. For example, to sign "black," a left-handed signer would slide the left pointer finger across the forehead to the left.

Some signs use the handshape for the letter the word begins with to make the sign. These are called initialized signs. Many of the signs for colors are initialized signs, including blue, brown, green, pink, purple, and yellow!

6 7 8 9 10

Signing Activities

Create a Deck of Cards: Get some blank index cards. On the front of each card, write the word for one color from the ASL glossary and draw a picture of something that color. Leave the back of each card blank. Repeat these steps until you have made two cards for each color mentioned in the book. Use your homemade deck of cards to help you learn and practice new signs.

Play "Go Fish": Shuffle your homemade cards and deal five cards to each player. Place the remaining cards facedown in a pile. The game's object is to get the most matching pairs. Players take turns signing to see if their partner has a card of a particular color. If the partner has a card that matches the sign, he must give it to the first player. If the partner does not have that card, he says, "Go fish," and the first player takes a card from the pile. Play continues until all the cards in the pile are gone.

Guess the Mystery Person: Get a group of friends to play together in a circle. Select someone to be the first signer. The signer secretly chooses someone within the circle to be the mystery person. The signer uses color signs to give the group three clues about what the mystery person is wearing. When another player thinks they know who the mystery person is, they raise their hand and the signer calls on them. If a player's guess is wrong, they must sit down and cannot guess again. The first player who correctly guesses the mystery person becomes the next signer and the game starts over. If all players are sitting and the mystery person still hasn't been identified, the signer points to the mystery person and that player becomes the next signer.

Additional Resources

Further Reading

Costello, Elaine, PhD. *Random House Webster's Concise American Sign Language Dictionary*. Bantam, 2002.

Heller, Lora. *Sign Language for Kids*. Sterling, 2004.

Sign2Me. *Pick Me Up! Fun Songs for Learning Signs (A CD and Activity Guide)*. Northlight Communications, 2003.

Warner, Penny. *Signing Fun*. Gallaudet University Press, 2006.

Web Sites

To learn more about ASL, visit ABDO Group online at **www.abdopublishing.com**. Web sites about ASL are featured on our Book Links page. These links are routinely monitored and updated to provide the most current information available.